**FRIENDS
OF ACPL**

THE FAT CAT

A DANISH FOLKTALE

Translated and illustrated

by JACK KENT

Parents' Magazine Press • New York

TO THE DANES IN MY LIFE

There was once an old woman who was
cooking some gruel. She had some
business with a neighbor woman
and asked the cat if he would look after
the gruel while she was gone.
"I'll be glad to," said the cat.

But when the old woman had gone,
the gruel looked so good that
the cat ate it all.

And the pot, too.

When the old woman came back,
she said to the cat, "Now what
has happened to the gruel?"

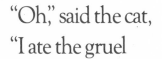

"Oh," said the cat,
"I ate the gruel
and I ate the pot, too.
And now I am going to also eat YOU."

And he ate the old woman.

He went for a walk and on the way
he met Skohottentot.

And Skohottentot said to him,
"What have you been eating,
my little cat? You are so fat."

And the cat said,
"I ate the gruel
and the pot
and the old woman, too.
And now I am going
to also eat YOU."

So he ate Skohottentot.

Afterwards he met Skolinkenlot.
Skolinkenlot said, "What have you
been eating, my little cat?
You are so fat."

"I ate the gruel
and the pot
and the old woman, too,
and Skohottentot," said the cat.
"And now I am going
to also eat YOU."

So he ate Skolinkenlot.

Next he met five birds in a flock.
And they said to him, "What have you
been eating, my little cat? You are so fat."

"I ate the gruel
and the pot
and the old woman, too,
and Skohottentot
and Skolinkenlot.
And now I am going
to also eat YOU."

And he ate the five birds in a flock.

Later he met seven girls dancing. And they, too, said to him,
"Gracious! What have you been eating, my little cat?
You are so fat."

And the cat said,
"I ate the gruel
and the pot
and the old woman, too,
and Skohottentot
and Skolinkenlot
and five birds in a flock.
And now I am going
to also eat YOU."

And he ate the seven girls dancing.

When he had gone a little farther,
he met a lady with a pink parasol.
And she, too, said to him,
"Heavens! What have you been eating,
my little cat? You are so fat."

"I ate the gruel
and the pot
and the old woman, too,
and Skohottentot
and Skolinkenlot
and five birds in a flock
and seven girls dancing.
And now I am going
to also eat YOU."

And he ate the lady
with the pink parasol.

A little later he met a parson with a crooked staff.

"Dear me! What have you been eating, my little cat?
You are so fat."

"Oh," said the cat,
"I ate the gruel
and the pot
and the old woman, too,
and Skohottentot
and Skolinkenlot
and five birds in a flock
and seven girls dancing
and the lady with the pink parasol.
And now I am going
to also eat YOU."

And he ate the parson with the crooked staff.

Next he met a woodcutter with an axe.

"My! What have you been eating, my little cat! You are so fat."

"I ate the gruel
and the pot
and the old woman, too,
and Skohottentot
and Skolinkenlot
and five birds in a flock
and seven girls dancing
and the lady with the pink parasol
and the parson with the crooked staff.
And now I am going
to also eat YOU."

"No. You are wrong, my little cat," said the woodcutter.

He took his axe
and cut the cat open.
And out jumped
the parson with the crooked staff
and the lady with the pink parasol

and the seven girls dancing
and the five birds in a flock
and Skolinkenlot
and Skohottentot.

U.S. 1712444

And the old woman took her pot
and her gruel and went home with them.

In addition to *The Fat Cat*, which Jack Kent translated from the Danish, Parents' Magazine Press has published four books written and illustrated by him: *Just Only John*, *The Grown-Up Day*, *The Blah*, and *Mr. Meebles*.

Jack Kent is a free-lance commercial artist and the creator of the comic strip, *King Aroo*. He was born in Burlington, Iowa, and, because his family traveled constantly, attended schools in many cities and states. He was living in San Antonio, Texas, when a local newspaper sent a reporter to interview him. He married the reporter.

The Kents live in San Antonio with their son. Incidentally, Jack, Jr. is talented in art, also, and when he was barely thirteen, he illustrated a story, written by his father, for *Humpty Dumpty's Magazine*.